Tanya
and the Geese

Tanya
and the Geese

By Jane Werner Watson

Drawings by June Goldsborough

GARRARD PUBLISHING COMPANY
CHAMPAIGN, ILLINOIS

Tanya
and the Geese

"The geese are out!
The geese are out!"
Tanya heard
her mother call.
"Oh, dear!" said Tanya.
"I left the gate open."

Tanya ran
to the open gate.
She could see
the geese, in a line,
waddling down the road.

Tanya ran
out the gate
and down the road.
She ran
after the fat white geese.

Her friend Greta saw her.

"What's the matter?"

Greta called.

"The geese are out!"

Tanya cried.

"I must get them back
or we will have
no feathers
for new feather beds."
"I will help you,"
called Greta.
Greta ran
down the road after Tanya.

Waddle, waddle,
the fat white geese
followed the gander
down the road.
Their toes pointed out.
Their beaks
were high in the air.
Tanya ran after them.
Her long braids flew.
Her striped apron blew.
Greta ran after Tanya.
Her pretty curls blew.
Her flowered apron flew.

Their friend Jan
was pulling his small cart
down the road.
He saw Tanya and Greta
running after the geese.
"What's the matter?"
Jan called.
"The geese are out!

We must get them back
or there will be
no feathers
for new feather beds,"
cried Tanya and Greta.
"I will help you,"
called Jan.
He ran down the road.

Pulling his small cart
behind him,
he ran
after Tanya and Greta.
Waddle, waddle,
the fat white gander
led the fat geese
faster and faster
down the road.
Around a corner
they went.
Tanya and Greta
ran after them.
Jan, pulling his small cart,
ran down the road
after Tanya and Greta.

His friend Babin saw him.

Babin was riding

in the back

of his father's wagon.

The wagon

was piled high

with round loaves of bread.

"What's the matter?"
called Babin.
"The geese are out.
We must get them back
or there will be no feathers
for new feather beds,"
said Jan.

"I will help you,"
called Babin.
So Babin jumped down
from the wagon,
with a round loaf of bread
still in his arms.
He ran down the road
after Tanya and Greta and Jan.
Waddle, waddle,
the fat white gander
led the fat geese
away from the road
into a big field
of sunflowers.
"Oh, dear!" cried Tanya
as she ran after them.

The stiff leaves
of the tall sunflowers
reached out.
The leaves tangled
her long braids.
Greta came after her.
She freed Tanya's braids
from the sunflower leaves.

Now they could not see
the geese!
Jan came after them.
He pulled his small cart
down the rows
of sunflower plants.
He could not see the geese.
Babin came after them,
with the round loaf of bread
still in his arms.
He could not see the geese.
"Oh, dear!" cried Tanya.
"We must get the geese back,
or there will be
no feathers
for new feather beds."

"Let's go to the pond
beyond the sunflower field,"
said Babin.
So Tanya led the way
through the sunflower field
to the pond.

Tanya held her long braids
to keep the stiff leaves
from catching them.
Greta followed Tanya
through the sunflower field.
She held her pretty curls
to keep the stiff leaves
from catching them.

Still pulling his cart,
Jan followed Greta.
Babin, still holding
his round loaf of bread
in his arms,
followed Jan.
Beyond the sunflower field
they came to the pond.
There were the geese,
swimming on the pond.

"Oh, dear!" said Tanya.
"See the big, sticky burdocks!"
The burdocks
with sticky prickers
grew along the pond.

"See the goose feathers
sticking on the burdocks!"
cried Greta.

Tanya and Greta

ran to the burdocks.

They picked off the feathers.

They piled the feathers
in their aprons.
Soon their aprons
were full of goose feathers.
Jan, still pulling his cart,
came after Tanya and Greta.

They shook their aprons
into the cart.
Soon it was full
of white goose feathers.

Babin came after Jan.
He was still holding
his round loaf of bread
in his arms.

"How can we make
the geese go home?"
asked Tanya.
"They do not want
to leave the pond,"
said Greta.

"They should be hungry,"
said Babin. He broke
his loaf of bread in half.
He tore off
small bits of bread.
"Here, geese! Here, geese!"
called Babin.

But the geese
did not come.
They swam
round and round
in the pond.

They paddled
with their feet.
They held their beaks
high in the air.
"Here, geese!
Here, geese!"
called Jan.

He held out
some bits of bread.
But the geese
did not come.
They just swam
round and round
in the pond.
"Here, geese!
Here, geese!"
called Greta.
She held out
some bits of bread.
But still
the geese did not come.
"I know those geese,"
said Tanya.

"I know
that fat white gander."
She took
some bits of bread.
She walked
around the burdocks
to the far side
of the pond.

She walked close
to the edge
of the water.
She leaned over
until her apron
almost touched the water.

Tanya held out
the bits of bread.
She held them
close to the beak
of the fat white gander.
"Here, dear gander,"
she said to him.
"Please bring
your silly geese this way.
There will be bits of bread
for you all."
The gander
opened his beak.
Tanya dropped
a bit of bread in.
She stepped back.

Then she dropped
another bit of bread
on the grass
at the edge of the pond.
The gander swam over.

He reached out
with his long neck.
He could not reach
the bit of bread.
Then he paddled
with his feet.
He stepped out
onto the grass.

He shook himself all over.
The drops of water flew!

Then he dipped
his long neck
and snapped up
the bit of bread.
The geese saw him eating.
They paddled
with their feet.

They swam
to the edge
of the pond.
Tanya walked slowly
away from the pond.
She dropped bits of bread
along the way.
Soon all the geese
were following her.

They dipped
their long necks
and snapped up the bread
with their beaks.
After the geese
came Greta,
waving a stick
to keep them in line.

After Greta came Jan,
still pulling his cart
of goose feathers.

After Jan came Babin,
still holding the other half
of his round loaf of bread.
Tanya led the way
down the lane
beside the sunflower field.

She led
the way down the road
back toward her own gate.
After her came the geese,
still snapping up
bits of bread.

After the geese
came Greta,
still waving her stick
to keep them in line.

After Greta came Jan,
still pulling his cart
of goose feathers.
After Jan came Babin,
still holding the other half
of his loaf of bread.

Tanya's mother was waiting
at the gate.
"Tanya!" called her mother.
"What is the matter
with the geese?

They have all lost
so many feathers!
Now there will be
no feathers
for new feather beds."
"Oh, yes,
there will be,"
said Tanya.

She led
the fat white gander
and the fat geese
into the yard.
After them came Greta,
still waving her stick
to keep them in line.

After Greta came Jan,
still pulling his small cart
of white goose feathers.
"Here are the feathers,"
said Tanya.

After Jan came Babin,
still holding
the other half
of his loaf of bread.
"Well," said Tanya's mother.
"Now I can make
the feather beds.
Come into the house,
all of you," she said.
She closed the gate
behind them.
She filled a pitcher
from the bucket
at the well.
She made them all
wash their faces and hands.

Then she fed them
bread and jam and milk.
Tanya's mother
thanked Greta and Jan.

They started to go home.
Greta was still waving
her stick.
Jan was still pulling
his small cart.
But it was empty now.

Tanya's mother thanked Babin.
She gave him
a new round loaf of bread.
Then Tanya's father
hitched up his wagon.
He started off
with Babin on the seat
beside him.

As for Tanya,
she stayed home.
She helped her mother
air the goose feathers
for the new feather beds.